VEGETABLES

in the Garden

Created by Pascale de Bourgoing
and Gallimard Jeunesse
Illustrated by Gilbert Houbre

A FIRST DISCOVERY BOOK

Cartwheel
·B·O·O·K·S· ®

SCHOLASTIC INC.
New York   Toronto   London   Auckland   Sydney

Vegetables are
plants. Their roots,
leaves, seeds, stems,
or flowers are eaten
as food.

Let's take
a look at
some delicious
garden
vegetables.

Peeled and sliced,
they are crunchy
and sweet to eat.
They're good for
you, too!

Carrots taste as good as they look!

Carrot plants
have roots,
stems, leaves, and flowers.
We eat the root
of the carrot plant —
the part that grows underground.

Tiny carrot seeds form
from the flowers of
the carrot plant.
The seeds are planted
in the ground.
It takes about 100 days
for a carrot to grow.

You can buy carrots like this — by the bunch, frozen, canned ...

and eat them raw or cooked; in soups or in cakes.

Carrots are filled with vitamins A and C,
which are good for your eyes and skin.

Radishes, celeriac,
and beets
are root vegetables, too.

We eat radishes raw.
Beets are always cooked.
Celeriac is a
kind of celery.
You can eat the root
cooked or raw.

Turnips, leeks, and onions
grow underground. We eat
the root of the turnip, the
stalk of the leek, and the
bulb of the onion plant.

Let's
look
inside
these
vegetables.

These taste
delicious in soup.
But watch out!
Raw onions make
your eyes water.

Potatoes were first grown
by the Incas of South America.
These Native Americans
called them *batatas*.

Here's how potatoes grow.

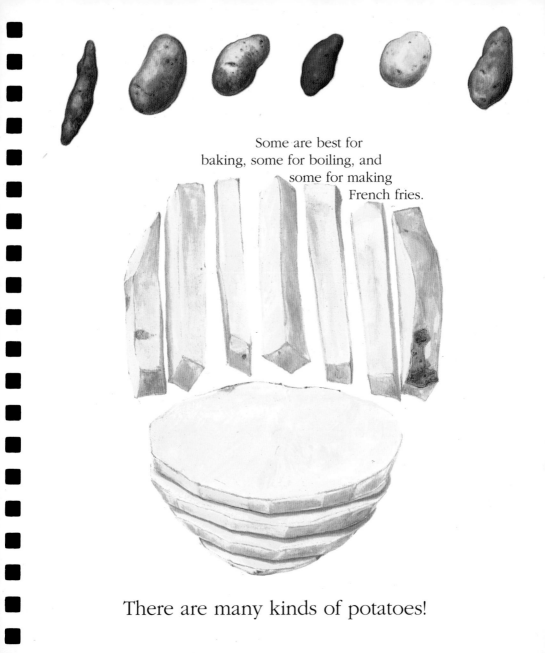

Some are best for
baking, some for boiling, and
some for making
French fries.

There are many kinds of potatoes!

Green cabbage

Cauliflower

These leafy vegetables
all grow above the ground.
Some we eat cooked and
some we eat raw in salads.

Red cabbage

Brussels sprouts

Leaf lettuce

Boston lettuce

Leaf vegetables start as
tiny sprouts. In a few weeks,
the fully grown leaves are ready
to eat! The leaves are filled with
B vitamins and vitamin A.

Spinach

Parsley

Eggplants, tomatoes,
and zucchini
all grow on vines.
They need warm
sunshine to grow.

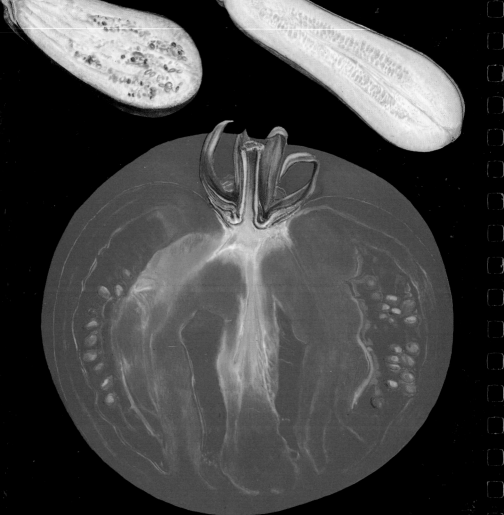

Can you see the tiny seeds?

We call these vegetables, but they are really fruits.

Green beans,
peppers, and
cucumbers
are also fruits
of the plant.

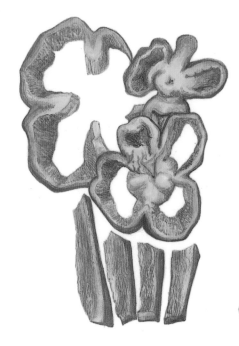

Inside the fruit are the seeds, which are needed to grow new plants.

Look at the seeds in this cucumber!

Peas and artichokes
grow above the ground.
Artichokes are the budding flowers
of the artichoke plant.
We eat the tender heart
of the artichoke.

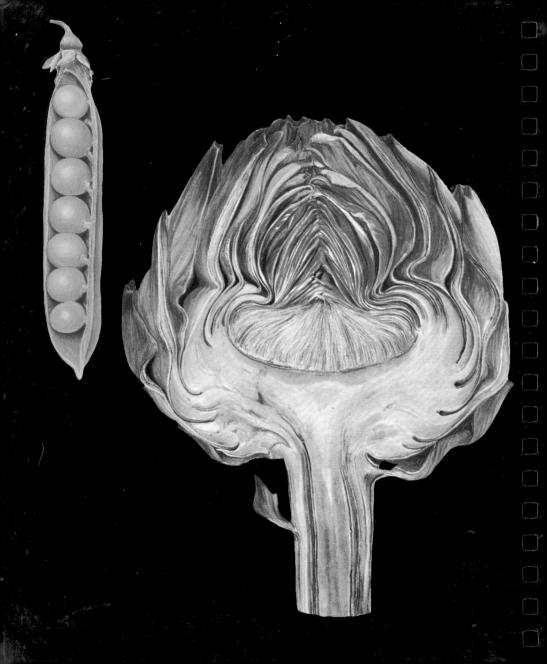

Let's look inside.

We eat
the seeds
inside
the pea pod.

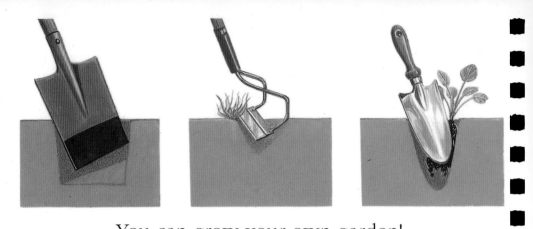

You can grow your own garden!

Find a sunny patch of land
with rich soil.
Use a spade to dig a hole.
Plant your seeds or seedlings
according to the directions
on the seed pack or label.
Be sure to water your plants.
And be patient.
A salad you grow yourself
is worth waiting for!

Titles in the series of *First Discovery Books:*

**Airplanes
and Flying Machines**
Bears
Birds
Winner, 1993
Parents Magazine
"Best Books" Award
Boats
Winner, 1993
Parents Magazine
"Best Books" Award
The Camera
Winner, 1993
Parents Magazine
"Best Books" Award
Castles
Winner, 1993
Parents Magazine
"Best Books" Award

Cats
Colors
Dinosaurs
The Earth and Sky
The Egg
Winner, 1992
Parenting Magazine
Reading Magic Award
Flowers
Fruit
**The Ladybug and
Other Insects**
Light
Musical Instruments
The Rain Forest
The River
Winner, 1993
Parents Magazine
"Best Books" Award

The Tree
Winner, 1992
Parenting Magazine
Reading Magic Award
**Vegetables in the
Garden**
Weather
Winner,
Oppenheim Toy Portfolio
Gold Seal Award
Whales
Winner, 1993
Parents Magazine
"Best Books" Award

Library of Congress Cataloging-in-Publication Data available.

Originally published in France under the title *La Carotte* by Editions Gallimard.

ISBN 0-590-48326-9

Copyright © 1989 by Editions Gallimard.
This edition English translation by Jennifer Riggs.
This edition American text by Nancy Krulik.
All rights reserved. First published in the U.S.A. in 1994 by Scholastic Inc., by arrangement with Editions Gallimard.
CARTWHEEL BOOKS ® is a registered trademark of Scholastic Inc.
12 11 10 9 8 7 6 5 4 3 2 1   4 5 6 7 8 9/9
Printed in Italy.
First Scholastic printing, September 1994